Princess Ava & the Daily Routine

Carmen Jones-Dobbins

AuthorHouse™
1663 Liberty Drive
Bloomington, IN 47403
www.authorhouse.com
Phone: 833-262-8899

Because of the dynamic nature of the Internet, any web addresses or links contained in this book may have changed
since publication and may no longer be valid. The views expressed in this work are solely those of the author and do not
necessarily reflect the views of the publisher, and the publisher hereby disclaims any responsibility for them.

Any people depicted in stock imagery provided by Getty Images are models,
and such images are being used for illustrative purposes only.
Certain stock imagery © Getty Images.

This book is printed on acid-free paper.

ISBN: 978-1-6655-7567-6 (sc)
ISBN: 978-1-6655-7568-3 (e)

Library of Congress Control Number: 2022920990

Print information available on the last page.

Published by AuthorHouse 11/16/2022

authorHOUSE®

Princess Ava & the Daily Routine

Dedication

To my family, my mom - Bonnie Cheatham, husband - Dr. Charles Dobbins Jr. and my children Charles III, Chris & Candice, thank you for believing in me!

To my most amazing first and only granddaughter, Ava, this book is for you and about you. I have enjoyed all the days we have spent together! You will always be my #Mimisgirl!

Love you all - Carmen, Ava's Mimi

Everyday Princess Ava has the same routine. Wake up, snuggle, potty time, brush teeth, and eat. When Princess Ava is sleeping so peacefully in her bed she is awakened by Mimi, the old woman in the castle.

The old woman asks the Princess what she would like to do? Princess Ava always replies "sleep in your bed". So, the old woman, pulls back the covers to her lowly bed and takes the little princess in and snuggles.

Princess Ava asks "can I watch my favorite show," Mimi, the old woman in the castle, grabs the remote and plays the princesses favorite show.

Soon after, Mimi, the old woman in the castle, says to the Princess, "time to go to the bathroom and start your morning routine".

Princess Ava is a big girl now and can do so much by herself. She is so **proud**. Princess Ava gets her big girl stool, places it at the sink, then she gets her toothbrush and toothpaste out and puts toothpaste on her toothbrush. She brushes her teeth so well that Mimi, the old woman in the castle, just checks her teeth to make sure they are sparkling clean, like a princesses teeth should.

As the daily routine progresses, Princess Ava checks her royal wardrobe and brings them to Mimi, the old woman in the castle. Mimi is the Princesses royal helper, she makes sure that the Princess always looks her best.

9

After Princess Ava is completely dressed she calls for the royal helper, Mimi. She says to Mimi, the royal helper, "it's time to go to the royal mirror". The royal mirror is where Princess Ava turns Mimi, the old woman and royal helper, into a beautiful queen.

10

Princess Ava steps up to the royal mirror and says "a wish I wish, not for a frog or a fish, but a beautiful queen for my Mimi to be, SWISH, SWISH"!

Then suddenly, a whirlwind appears, surrounding Mimi, the old woman and royal helper to the Princess. The cloud completely covers Mimi from head to toe and then, just as the cloud begins to disappear, you can see the beautiful, amazing transformation, a queen. Mimi is no longer the old woman in the castle or the royal helper to the princess, but she is a beautiful queen!

13

Princess Ava and Queen Mimi look in the royal mirror, and with a SWISH SWISH, they start their day in the royal kingdom of Dobbs.

Dobbs

15

Proud - to be very happy about something you have done.

Printed in the United States
by Baker & Taylor Publisher Services